This Boxer Books paperback belongs to

. . . .

www.boxerbooks.com

For The Muss
Sam Williams

For my lovely daughter, Maja
Cecilia Johansson

First published in hardback in Great Britain in 2016 by Boxer Books Limited.

First published in paperback in Great Britain in 2017 by Boxer Books Limited.

www.boxerbooks.com

Boxer® is a registered trademark of Boxer Books Limited

A catalogue record of this book is available from the British Library.

The illustrations were prepared digitally.

The text is set in Adobe Garamond Pro

ISBN 978-1-910716-03-8

1 3 5 7 9 10 8 6 4 2

Printed in China

All of our papers are sourced from managed forests and renewable resources.

Croc? What Croc?

Written by Sam Williams

Illustrated by Cecilia Johansson

Boxer Books

Little Fluff sauntered by the river. He was on his way to meet a friend for a picnic.

"Croc!" shouted Flamingo.
Little Fluff looked puzzled.

"Croc? What croc?"
said Little Fluff, skipping
over a rock and laughing.

"Croc!"
shouted Monkey.
Little Fluff looked around.

"Croc? What croc?"
asked Little Fluff,
flying through the air.

"Croc!"

shouted Elephant.

"Croc? What croc?" asked Little Fluff, leaping over a big, muddy hole.

"Gorilla!"

Little Fluff shouted.

"Crocodile!"
shouted Gorilla.

"Arghhhhhh," screamed Crocodile, "Gorilla!" and jumped into the river.

Gorilla scooped Little Fluff
up with his big, strong arms.
"Hello, Little Fluff. I didn't know
you were bringing a friend."
"I wasn't," laughed Little Fluff.

So Little Fluff and Gorilla sat down on the riverbank and had the most wonderful picnic – just the two of them . . . without a croc in sight!

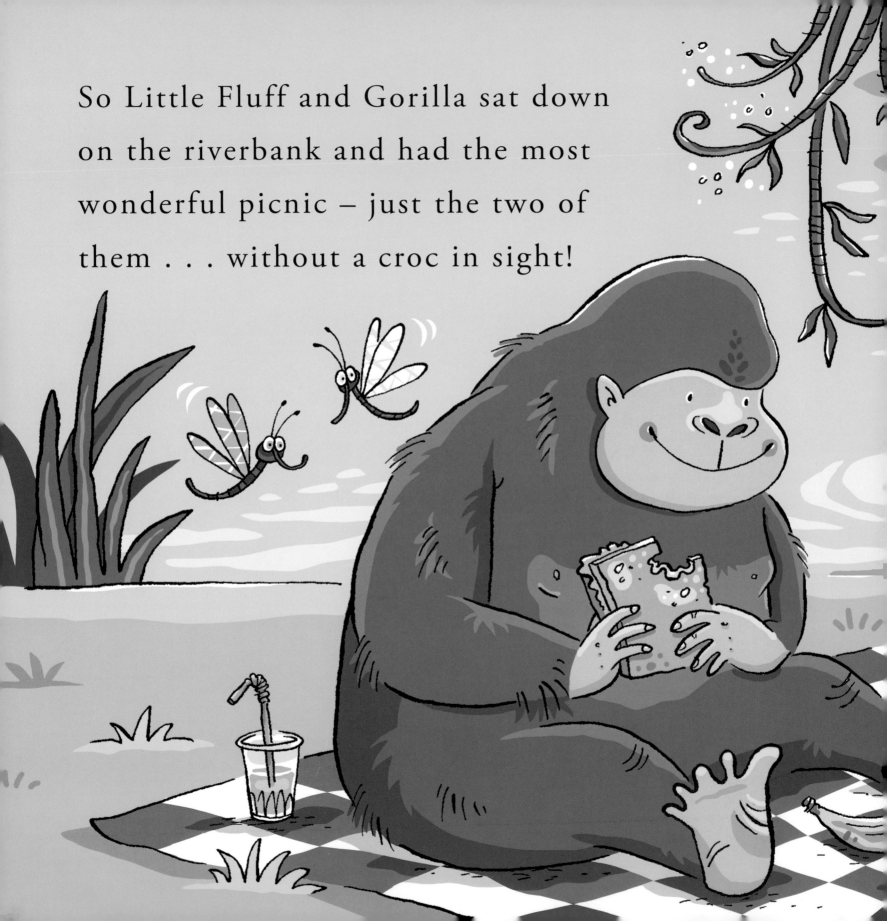

More Boxer Books to enjoy

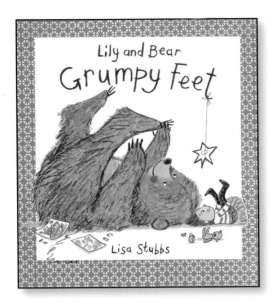

Lily and Bear: Grumpy Feet
by Lisa Stubbs
Something is not right. The day is too rainy, the teapot too dribbly and Lily's sunshine colour is missing from her crayons. Oh no, she's woken up with Grumpy Feet! What can her best friend Bear do to turn the grumps back into the jumps?

How Much Does a Ladybird Weigh?
by Alison Limentani
Have you ever wondered how much a ladybird weighs? What about the weight of a snail, a bird or even a swan? An extraordinary and original picture book that introduces you to a fascinating world of numbers, weight and wildlife.

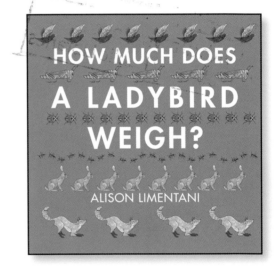

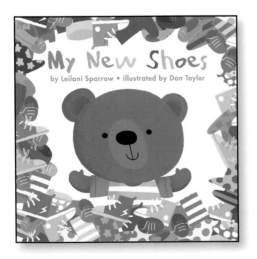

My New Shoes
by Leilani Sparrow
Illustrated by Dan Taylor
A simple introduction to buying a new pair of shoes. Short, fun and effective text with lots of rhythm and adorable animal characters to share the experience.